WHERE'S GOD WHEN I'M S-SCARED?

Adapted by Karen Poth
Illustrated by Paul Conrad

Based on the VeggieTales® video *Where's God When I'm S-Scared?*, written by Phil Vischer

A GOLDEN BOOK • NEW YORK

Library of Congress Control Number: 2006936527   ISBN: 978-0-375-83931-3
www.goldenbooks.com
www.randomhouse.com/kids
Printed in the United States of America
10 9 8 7 6 5 4 3 2 1

"**JUNIOR!** It's time for bed," Mom Asparagus called out from the kitchen. "Besides, that *Tales from the Crisper* TV show is too scary for you."

"I'm not s-s-scared," Junior answered as he climbed the stairs.

In the darkness of his bedroom, Junior sat in his bed with his eyes wide open. "I'm not s-s-scared," he repeated to himself as he pulled the covers up to his nose.

But he *was* scared.
He was scared of every
shadow in his room and
every noise in the hall.

KERPLUNK! Suddenly, a big red monster jumped right onto Junior's bed!

"I'm Bob," the monster said. "I'm a tomato, and I'm here to help you."

Then, **WHAM!** Junior's toy chest flew open, and out popped . . . a baby pickle?

"I'm Larry. I'm a cucumber. And I'm here to help you, too!" the cucumber said.

They were unlike any monsters Junior had ever seen. Then the cucumber and the tomato began to SING!

You were lying in
your bed.
You were feeling
kind of sleepy.
But you couldn't
close your eyes
Because the room
was getting
CREEPY.

Were those
EYEBALLS
in the closet?

Was that **GODZILLA**
in the hall?

There was something **BIG AND HAIRY**
casting shadows on the wall!

DON'T BE AFRAID!

God is bigger than the boogeyman.
He's bigger than Godzilla
or the monsters on TV.

*Oh, God is bigger than the boogeyman
and He's watchin' out for you and me!*

"Do you get it?" Bob asked. "You don't have to be afraid, because God is the BIGGEST!"
"Bigger than King Kong?" asked Junior.
"Because King Kong's a *really* big monkey!"

"Next to God, King Kong looks like an itty-bitty toy!" Larry said.

"Is He bigger than the Slime Monster?" Junior asked. "Because that's the biggest monster of them all!"

"Compared to God, the Slime Monster is a teeny cornflake," Larry said.

Bob and Larry took Junior over to the window.

"Just look at the sky!" Larry told Junior. "God made all those stars out of nothing."

"Wow!" Junior said. "The Slime Monster can't do *that*!"

"And God made the animals and all the people, too!" Bob continued. "We don't have to be afraid, because God watches out for everything He made."

"So God's the biggest of all, and He's on my team!" Junior shouted.

"Hey! What's all the racket?"
Junior's dad asked, peeking in.

"Oh, I was just singing a little song," Junior said. "God is bigger than any monster! He made the whole world, and He takes good care of me, too!"

"That's right," Junior's dad agreed. "Now get some sleep."

And then, in the dark, Junior fell fast asleep. He wasn't scared, because he knew that God was right there with him.